Affections Offering

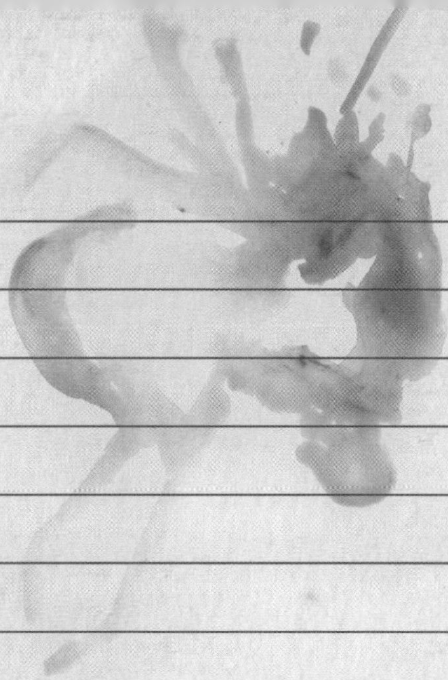

CRUMP!

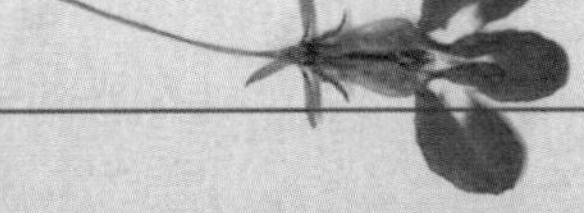

CRUMP!

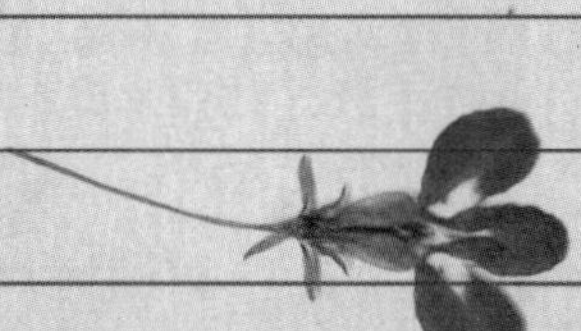

Affections Offering

CRUMP!

CRUMP!

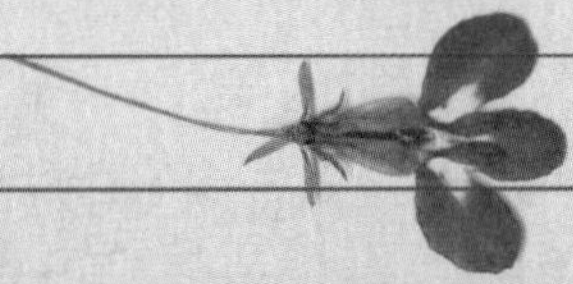

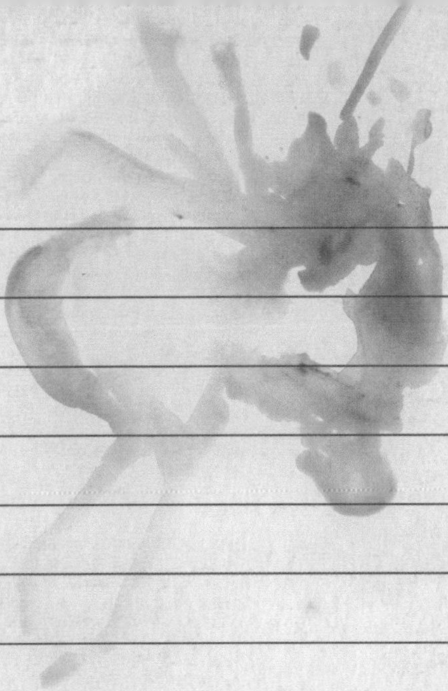

CRUMP!

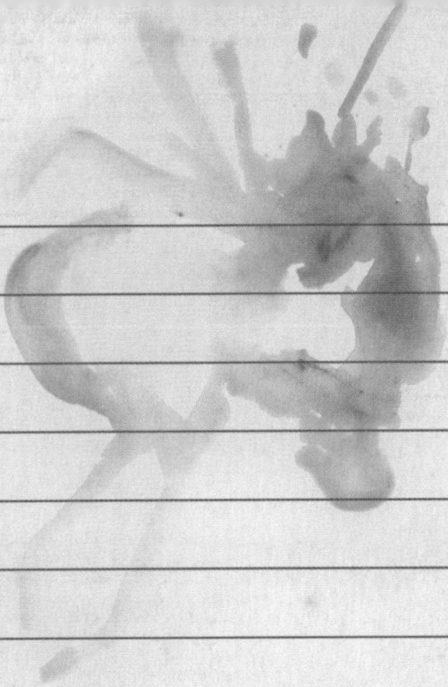

CRUMP!

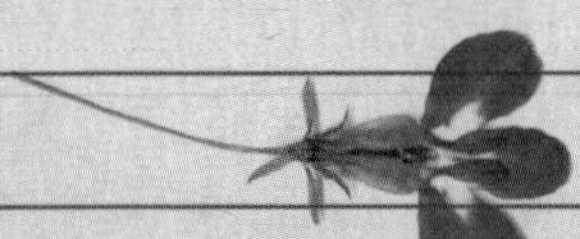

CRUMP!

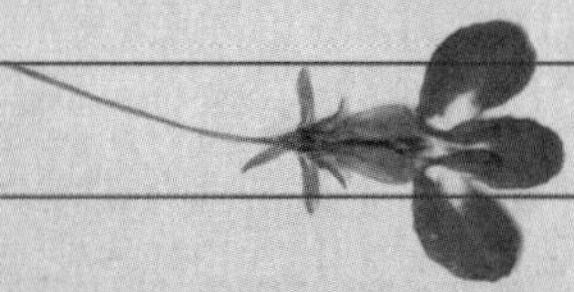

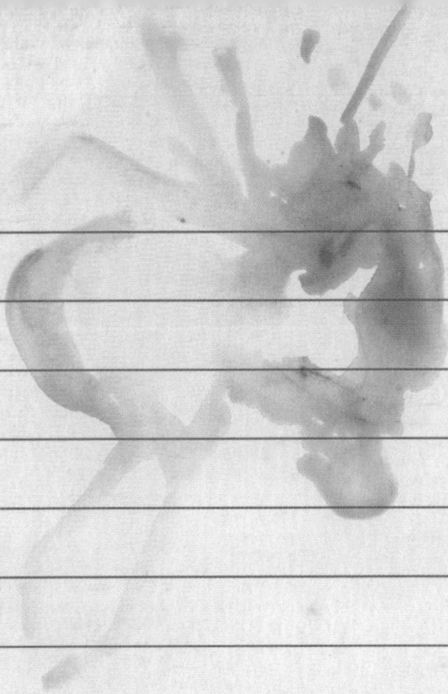

CRUMP!

Affections Offering

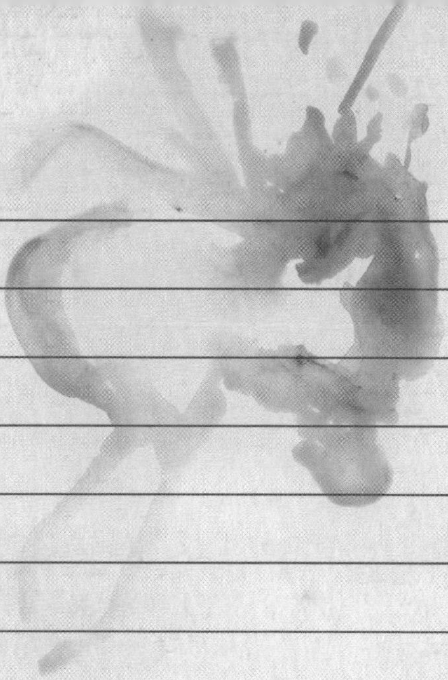

CRUMP!

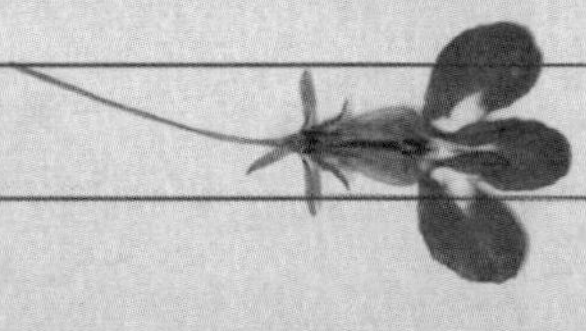

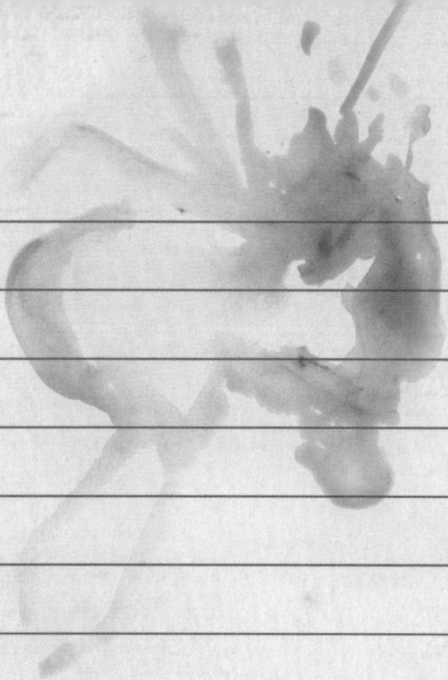

Crump!

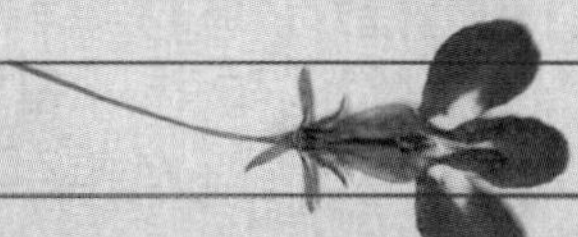

Affections Offering

CRUMP!

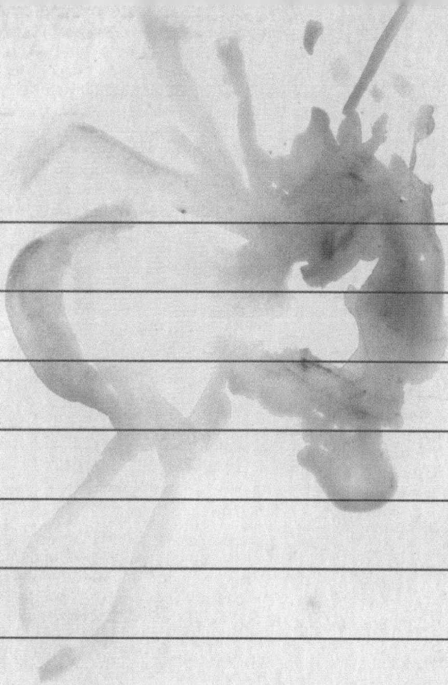

CRUMP!

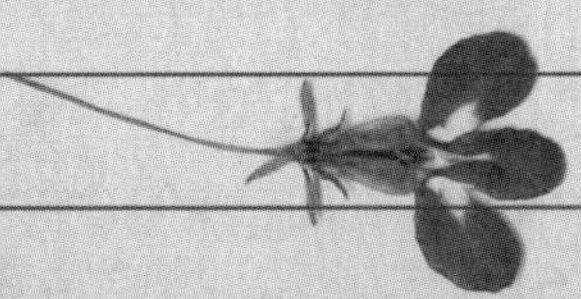